HELPER HOUNDS

Sparky

Helps Mary Make New Friends

Dedication
To the fine folks at Hinsdale Humane Society,
thanks for loving Rocky, Blade, and Sierra
until we could call them ours.

In memory of
Carla Fisher
The best dog trainer ever
Your amazing advice lives on.

HELPER HOUNDS

Sparky

Helps Mary Make New Friends

Caryn Rivadeneira
Illustrated by Priscilla Alpaugh

RED
CHAIR
·PRESS·

Egremont, Massachusetts

RED CHAIR PRESS
BOOKS FOR YOUNG READERS

www.redchairpress.com

 Free educator's guide at www.redchairpress.com/free-resources

Publisher's Cataloging-In-Publication Data
Names: Rivadeneira, Caryn Dahlstrand, author. | Alpaugh, Priscilla, illustrator.
Title: Sparky helps Mary make new friends / Caryn Rivadeneira ; illustrated by Priscilla Alpaugh.

Description: [Egremont, Massachusetts] : Red Chair Press, [2020] | Series: Helper hounds | Interest age level: 006-009. | Includes fun facts and information about the mixed dog breed, Border collie and Bernese mountain dog. | Summary: "Mary's new in town and worried about starting classes at a new school. So her mom called the Helper Hounds--and that is why Sparkplug, the wildly handsome, wickedly smart, world famous Helper Hound is on the scene."--Provided by publisher.

Identifiers: ISBN 9781634407748 (library hardcover) | ISBN 9781634407779 (paperback) | ISBN 9781634407809 (ebook)

Subjects: LCSH: Mixed breed dogs--Juvenile fiction. | First day of school--Juvenile fiction. | Moving, Household--Juvenile fiction. | Friendship--Juvenile fiction. | CYAC: Dogs--Fiction. | First day of school--Fiction. | Moving, Household--Fiction. | Friendship--Fiction.

Classification: LCC PZ7.1.R5761 Sp 2020 (print) | LCC PZ7.1.R5761 (ebook) | DDC [E]--dc23

Library of Congress Control Number: 2019935132

Printed in Canada

0819 1P FRSP20

CHAPTER 1

I raced to Tasha's desk. I knew that *"bing!"* anywhere. It was the sound her computer made when we got a fresh case. I wagged my tail. It shook my whole body. I pressed my snout into Tasha's side.

"Easy, buddy," Tasha said.

I sat like a good dog. But I couldn't stop my tail. It swooshed across the wood floor. Dust bunnies hopped away as my tail swept. Sweeping floors is one of the *many* things I am great at.

My mouth opened into a huge smile. My tongue rolled out the side. I couldn't help that either. *Holy cow.* This was exciting!

"OK," Tasha said. "Looks like we've got a new assignment for you."

I knew it! *Tell me! Tell me! Who needs me?*

"There's a little girl named Mary," Tasha said.

Mary. Mary. I like her already! Tufts of hair flew off my tail. (I may have been drooling. But that's not important.)

"Her mom got a new job," Tasha said. Her eyes squinted at the screen. "The family just moved from Texas to Chicago. Mary's starting at a new school and is pretty nervous. She's worried about making new friends."

New job. Texas. Chicago. New school. New friends. Nervous. Got it!

"This sounds perfect for you, Sparkplug," Tasha said.

I barked and put my front paws on her lap.

"Yeah, Spark, you know all about moving and new homes and new friends, don't you?"

I barked again. I do. I know all about moving. Plus, another thing I'm great at? Meeting new friends. I can help Mary with that, no problem.

"Should I say yes to this one, Spark?"

My bottom wagged along with my tail. I barked twice.

"I'll take that as a yes," Tasha said.

Tasha is good at reading my mind. She knows me well.

So our next adventure was about to begin. Tasha plunked on the keyboard and grabbed my red Helper Hound vest and name badge. My mission to help Mary with her new school jitters and make new friends was launching in 3-2-1...!

CHAPTER 2

Before we go, perhaps I should tell you a bit about myself. This is how I became a world-famous, card-carrying Helper Hound.

I was born in a barn. My dad, Jasper, was a world-champion herding dog, a Border Collie from two farms over. He was great at rounding up sheep. Jasper was also good at roaming around the central Wisconsin farmlands.

That's where he met my mom, Betsy: a beautiful, prize-winning Bernese Mountain Dog, whose main job was to have puppies. Purebred Bernese Mountain Dog puppies, that is. Puppies, puppies, and more puppies.

You'd think the lady who fed my mom would've been happy when my brothers, sisters, and I came along. But she wasn't. Since our dad was a roaming Border Collie from two farms over and *not* a prize-winning Bernese Mountain Dog, Mom's lady sneered at us. She called us "mutts" and "mongrels." She never even pet us! Not that I remember.

As soon as we were "ready," which meant as soon as we were munching on puppy food and drinking water and sleeping away from Mom, the lady sent us all away. Normally she made people pay lots and lots of money for Mom's fancy puppies, but since we were "worthless mutts," she gave us to whomever would take us. For *free*.

My first family only kept me for a couple of weeks. Today, I'm a champ at pooping and peeing in the yard. That little corner behind the garage is my favorite spot. It's a fun surprise for the possums who walk back there. But when I was a little guy, I wasn't so good at it. After a couple of "accidents"—at least that's what humans call it, but I always remember peeing on purpose!—in the house, my first family decided I had to go. That's OK. Their carpet was starting to smell funny anyway.

So, off I went. This time, the family was a lot nicer. They admired my good looks. Which reminds me: have I already told you about my looks? My shiny black, brown, and white coat? The way my hair *flows* when I run? The way my white snout shows off the beautiful dirt I'm always rooting around in? Let's just say I'm really handsome. Everyone says so. Even strangers at the park who don't even know me.

And this family even understood my brains. Mutt or no mutt, I come from quality Border Collie stock, and Border Collies are the smartest dogs. Don't believe me? Google it.

That family talked about how good I'd be in obedience classes. I'd be some sort of champion at jumping through hoops and weaving around poles, they said. But they never signed me up for those classes. I stayed in the apartment day after day, locked in a crate, bored out of my mind.

I needed *something* to do. So I began tearing up the bedding and toys they put in my crate. I'd splash the water bowl on the floor around me. I'd pee and poop in my crate. Just to mix it up a little. A dog's gotta live!

And I kept growing. While I had my dad's brains, I had my mom's brawn. I got big. Too big for that crate. And too big to live in an apartment. At least, that's what the family said when they dropped me off at the shelter, where I stayed in a kennel day in and day out.

The shelter wasn't home, but it wasn't too bad. The people at the shelter were nice. They gave me fresh toys to play with and took me on long walks through woods on a hill. There were lots of other dogs to bark at. I pretended I was herding them all into that big outdoor kennel.

But it was lonely. The nights got long. All the dogs would howl and bark, hoping the workers and volunteers would come back. I'd just curl up and dream about rounding up sheep or helping humans. Something to use this big brain for.

Then one day Tasha showed up.

CHAPTER 3

Tasha walked up and down the walkway outside the kennels, looking at all the dogs, reading their descriptions:

> *7-year-old Shih Tzu-ish looking for a single adult to snuggle with.*
> *Not interested in kids or cats.*

> *4-year-old Mighty Mix looking for a sofa to sleep on.*
> *Good with cats, other dogs, and older kids.*

She stopped by me once. I sat my Good Dog Sit for her. I even stopped barking. Then I swished my tail to show her how good at sweeping I was. Tasha smiled, and I knew she was the human for me. And not just because her smile smelled like pizza. (But it did.)

Tasha had pulled her hair into a tail that day. It stuck straight out the back of her head. She carried a clipboard and took notes as she read my card:

9-month-old high-energy Border Collie mix looking for dedicated person.
Happy to spend the day working, playing with kids, or training for agility.
No cats need apply.

I could tell this woman meant business. I like business. It means work.

When Tasha walked on to the kennel next to me—where that Corker the Cocker Spaniel was always soaking her ears in her water bowl— I had to act. I couldn't let this one get away.

I barked. And barked and barked. If sitting

nicely and sweeping handily wasn't going to do it for her, maybe a little noise would.

"You have something more to say there, umm, Sparkplug, is it?"

Tasha came back!

I did! I did! I barked again and spun to the back end of my kennel to get my blue barbell.

"You like to play, do you?" Tasha asked.

I barked and dropped the barbell. *Holy cow!* You bet I did.

Tasha looked from side to side. I knew what she was doing. People weren't supposed to reach their hands into our cages, but they always did if no workers were around.

Then she reached under the cage and grabbed my barbell. I sat up straight, tongue out, eyes on the barbell. Tasha stood up, reached her arm over the kennel gate, and flung it to the back of my kennel.

I spun around, jumped, and grabbed it.

I trotted back and dropped my barbell at the kennel gate.

"You've got a good play drive," Tasha said. I didn't know what that was. But I barked. I'm sure I did. "I better see if I can get you outside."

Tasha bent down to rub my nose. I noticed her name tag: Helper Hounds, it said. It had her picture on it—along with another dog. The dog in the picture—all muscle and boxy-headed and short-haired—wore a red vest that said Helper Hounds on it.

I didn't know what a Helper Hound was. But I wanted in. It sounded like just the job for me. Sometimes people called me "hound dog," and I do like to help. (Remember my big brain?)

Anyway, Tasha took me outside and walked me. I lifted my leg and peed on my favorite oak, just so Tasha would see how good I was at going to the bathroom *outside*. Tasha laughed and said something about my impressive leg flexibility.

Then, Tasha ran me through all kinds of games of fetch. I don't mean to brag, but I was amazing. Not only can I catch *anything* you throw at me, but I can get it back to you faster than you can say, "Get it, Sparkplug."

Tasha "taught" me some tricks. (Full disclosure: I've *always* known how to sit, lie down, roll over, and sit pretty. But I let her think she was teaching me how to do it. I get better treats that way.) Then she introduced me to her niece and nephew. They walked me and pet me and asked me to sit too. I liked those kids. And they liked me. All the while, Tasha would write down stuff on her paper. She smiled the whole time. So did I.

Before I knew it, Tasha was taking me home. OK, OK, I was so excited that I peed on the floor a little bit. Right there in the lobby of the shelter. And then my tail flicked the puddle on Robin, my favorite friend there. But everyone just laughed and came out to hug and kiss and pet me goodbye. I'd made lots of friends at the shelter. They loved me. What can I say? I'm a very good boy and, as I mentioned, quite handsome.

Tasha took me to those obedience classes I'd heard so much about. No surprise: I was the best dog in my class. I could do everything and anything. *Sit. Stay. Sit-stay. Sit pretty. Heel. Here. Come. Down. Speak. Settle. Easy. Leave it.* And I could do them all while also giving Fluffernutter the Chihuahua my world-class stink eye. I knew how badly she wanted my jerky treats.

I graduated and went on to Canine Good Citizen classes. I was the best student there too. I got an award. After that, Tasha sent in my application—complete with a link to my Dog Tube account, which features videos of my skills—to Helper Hounds University.

A few weeks later, Tasha's computer binged. Tasha read me an email that told me I got in.

No surprise there. But Tasha cried and hugged me. She was so proud.

"Helper Hounds U is where dogs get their Helper Hounds magic," Tasha said.

I was pretty sure I already had magic. But I couldn't wait to start.

CHAPTER 4

I'm a brave dog. But I got nervous when Tasha parked the car outside Helper Hounds U. I saw the dogs sitting still as statues while a man weaved his wheelchair through them. When he'd stop quickly in front of a dog, none of them stretched forward to sniff the guy's knees. That is, until their person said, "OK." Then they leaned in and gave kisses and got pets. These dogs were *good*!

Tasha was nervous too. Did you know dogs can feel our people's emotions through a leash? Well, we can. Feelings like fear or joy, being nervous or relaxed, all travel through leashes— and even the air. It's weird but true!

Anyway, I almost *never* feel Tasha getting nervous, but as we trotted up to the fence where the dogs were, Tasha's jitters jolted into me. Helper Hounds U is a big deal. Dogs that don't pass these classes don't get to be Helper Hounds.

To remind Tasha that she was here with the mighty Sparkplug, all handsome and smart and brave, I sat my perfect Good Boy Sit. Still as a statue. Even when Mr. Tuttle, my professor, walked up.

"You must be Sparkplug," Mr. Tuttle said.

Mr. Tuttle smelled amazing, a mix of wet dog and hay, but also the pizza he had for lunch.

Tasha told me "OK," so I gave Mr. Tuttle my paw. Then I sat pretty for good measure. Mr. Tuttle knelt down to pet me. Then he gave me a big hug and held on for a while. I gave him two sniffs and then settled in. I don't mind big hugs, but lots of dogs hate them.

"Well done, Sparkplug," Mr. Tuttle said. "Good dog."

My mouth opened into my best smile.

Before taking me into the ring with the other dogs, Mr. Tuttle tested me on a couple of other exercises. Tasha said, "down," and I lied down. Then she said "side," so I rolled on to my side. Mr. Tuttle sat on the grass next to me, rubbed my belly (my favorite!), and put his head on my side and then leaned his whole body against mine.

Lots of dogs hate this too. I don't *love* it, but I don't mind. Not if it helps somebody feel better.

Mr. Tuttle petted me all over and told me what a good boy I was. He gave Tasha a thumbs-up and said, "I'm impressed."

Tasha grabbed my leash. I felt her joy. Then we went into the ring.

I met Robber first. Today, Robber and I are buddies. We've gone on a million adventures together. But when I first met Robber, I didn't know what to make of the guy. First of all, he's *huge*. Robber weighs 120 pounds. That's more than me and more than Tasha. Second of all, Robber smells like cows. No kidding! A dog that smells like a cow! Third of all, he's got a stubby little tail. This makes it hard to know if he's happy or nervous or just regular.

I could tell Mr. Tuttle was watching me closely though, so when Robber trotted up, I sat my Good Boy Sit. I let Robber sniff me first. Then I sniffed him. Cow, cow, and a little hint of…goose? Robber stretched his front feet forward and thrust his bottom in the air, launching into a play-bow. I followed. We had a great time jumping and slobbering on one another.

I only put my neck over his once or twice.

I just wanted to show him I *could* be boss if I wanted to. But I didn't want to be boss.
I wanted to be a Helper Hound.

After a couple of minutes, Tasha called me over and told me to sit. I did. Perfectly.

Then Peach came over. She was about my size and easy to read. Her tail wagged nonstop. It was almost embarrassing. I mean, I *know* it's great to meet me, but most dogs like to play it a little cooler than that.

Peach didn't care. She loved meeting new people and new dogs and was happy to show it. It made me feel great, actually.

Peach and I sniffed and sniffed and sniffed. She must have rolled in some fresh skunk grass. She smelled amazing. Then we jumped and jumped and wrestled a little. Her tail never once stopped wagging. When Tasha called me over, I was panting. My tongue drooped way out the side of my mouth. Peach's tongue drooped out too, but on her, it looked like a great big smile.

I met lots of other dogs that day too. Some dogs were new, just like me. Others, like Robber and Peach, had been Helper Hounds for a while. They came back to practice their skills.

At Helper Hounds U, we worked on commands like "leave it." This is very important. *Leave it* means no matter how good that tissue on the floor smells, we ignore it. Same goes for cans or boxes or clothes or toys or anything that smells great.

"Could be dangerous, Spark." That's what Tasha told me. I'm pretty sure I can smell danger, but she was only looking out for me, so I worked hard on ignoring everything on the ground. No matter how interesting it looked or smelled!

We worked on cool things like *listening* and *resting* and just being calm even when people were nervous.

We didn't just do our training on the farm,

either. Sometimes we went to airports and got on airplanes. Sometimes we went to shopping malls. Sometimes we went to schools or churches. Lots of times we went to hospitals and sat still and calm while alarms sounded and people rushed around and the air fizzled with nerves.

On my last day of Helper Hounds U, the day I took my big exam, Tasha brushed my hair and kissed my head. Tasha prayed "we" would be calm and do well so that we could help others. But I was already calm as could be.

Mr. Tuttle met us outside the ring. He had a clipboard and a pen in his hands. I could hear the scratch on the paper as I went through my exercises. Perfectly, I might add.

At the end of my exam, Mr. Tuttle nodded and went into the Helper Hounds office. He came back out with a red vest and a name tag in his hands.

"Congratulations, Tasha," Mr. Tuttle said. "You did a great job. He's wonderful."

Tasha knelt down and hugged me hard. Then she scratched me all over and reminded me what a Good Dog I was. As if I'd forgotten.

But I wanted Tasha to know what a Good Human she was, so I jumped and kissed her and wrapped my paws around her waist. Helper Hounds really weren't supposed to jump, but this was a party!

Tasha got a new name tag too: one with a picture of her and me on it this time.

Tasha cried when she put the old name tag—the one of her and a dog named Noser—in her drawer. But I knew just what to do. My very first job as an official, name-tag-wearing Helper Hound was to lean into Tasha as she cried. I snuggled close and then licked her face. She laughed. I barked. I helped!

Today, as a proud member of the Helper

Hounds, I travel all over the place—sometimes by car, sometimes by airplane, sometimes with Robber, Peach, and the other Helper Hounds, and sometimes with just Tasha. We help people who need a little love or encouragement or just a dog to cry on or to pet.

Being a Helper Hound is better than rounding up sheep all day. It's better than solving mysteries. Being a Helper Hound is the Best Job Ever. I get to do what I'm good at *and* I've learned so many cool tricks. Which I get to teach other people—like Mary! Let's get back to her story.

CHAPTER 5

I smelled the muffins before Tasha stopped the car. *Peanut Butter! Banana. Flour. Eggs.* All still warm.

Drool puddled on the seat in front of me.

"Oh, Sparky," Tasha said. She grabbed a towel and wiped my mouth. She'd already brushed my fur *and* my teeth before we left the house. "Good hygiene is good manners."

Good advice. But the reason I'm good at making friends isn't because my smile sparkles and my fur shines. I'm good at making friends because I make *other* people smile and *other* people shine.

Since people *do* smile when they see my shiny fur, I knew I'd teach Mary this trick.

I wanted to run straight to the door—to the muffins *and* to Mary. But Tasha had me on my leash. So after I stopped to pee on a nice patch of raccoon-scented grass, I walked nicely, right at her side, all the way to the big green door.

Tasha rang the bell. *Bing bong bing bong. Bong bing bong bing.*

I waited to hear a bark. I always bark at the bell. It's exciting. A doorbell means I'm about to charm some new friends.

No one barked. But someone did purr. *Uh oh.*

The hair down my spine stood straight up. Turns out the *only* creatures I'm not good at making friends with are cats. I don't know what it is about them, but cats *never* like me. Probably because they sense my smarts. Cats like to think they're smarter than dogs. They may be smarter than *some* dogs, but not this dog.

I sniffed under the door. The cat smelled young. And like peanut butter...muffins! Wait. Were those muffins for *her*? I was hoping they were for *me*!

"Coming!" a woman's voice yelled from inside. Feet shuffled on a carpet behind the green door.

I sat. My tail wagged.

The door opened.

A gray cat sat on the other side. Her green eyes lasered into mine.

My tail stopped wagging for one moment. But one moment only.

Because just behind the cat was Mary.

No matter how badly I wanted to chase this cat, or at least give her a little peek into my strong canine teeth, that wasn't a good model of making friends for Mary. And I was here for her. I was here to help Mary make friends.

And that green-eyed, peanut-butter-banana-muffin-smelling cat was going to help me do it.

CHAPTER 6

But first, I was going to help Mary *settle down*.
Relaxing and believing it's going to be OK is
the second trick for making new friends. When
we get too nervous, we forget to believe in
ourselves. That's why *settle down* is the second
trick for making new friends.

Humans don't usually know this, but dogs
can *smell* your nervousness. We can also hear
your heartbeats—especially when they speed up.
But smell is the main thing.

Fear and anxiety smell a little like sweat.
They smell a lot like gasoline. Like if you pump
gas into your car on a real hot day. Well, sort of.

It's hard to explain.

But anyway, that's what Mary smelled like when she walked into the hallway and shook Tasha's hand. More than the banana. More than the peanut butter. More than anything, I smelled Mary's nervousness. That's how I knew she needed to settle!

So I showed her how. My *settle* command has always been perfect, as you probably guessed.

I scooted in closer. Mary knelt down to pet me. I sat statue-still and slowed my panting—the perfect settle. But I swished my tail gently across the tile floor. *That* showed her the "It's gonna be OK" part. (My super-stiff tail tells you we've got something to worry about!)

"So you're the famous Sparkplug," Mary said.

Holy cow! Mary's voice was the best. Low with a little crackle. Like a young frog I caught once back on the farm.

I answered Mary with my paw and a snout-to-the-sky bark. This is always a crowd-pleaser.

The cat wasn't pleased, though. She slinked around the corner into the dining room. I sniffed after her. *Is that where the muffins are?*

I started to follow that cat, but Tasha called me into another room. Tasha sat on a cushy sofa.

I wanted to hop up next to her like I do at home. But when my vest is on, I stay on the floor. Those are the rules. According to Tasha, second impressions matter just as much as first ones.

Mary and her mom sat in high-back chairs across from us. Mary's leg bounced. Her fingers folded into each other, like she was praying.

Tasha pulled a folder out of our Helper Hounds bag and leaned it over to Mary. Every Helper Hounds visit starts with the folder. The folder is the most boring part of a Helper Hounds visit. I wish we could skip the "paperwork," as Tasha calls it, and just get to playing and snuggling together.

But Tasha says the folder is important. She reminded me of this when I rested my head on her knee and gave her "the look." Tasha thinks a scratch behind the ears is a good reminder to hold tight, to relax, and to do my Good Dog settle.

Tasha is right. Scratching *always* helps me be patient.

And that glossy 8 × 10 headshot of me inside that folder *is* really handsome. Like Movie Star Handsome. As Tasha talked and talked and talked and as Mary's mom sifted through the papers—pausing and smiling at the picture—and scratched a pen across a couple of the papers, my eyelids drooped. My body slid to the floor. My tags clanged on the wood floor between my paws.

I figured I might as well get a power-nap in and model some mindful relaxation for Mary.

"Is this boring?" I heard someone ask. Mary. She scooted up next to me and ran her hand down my back. I turned my head for a quick lick. *Blech.* Hand-sanitizer. Why humans insist on washing their hands so much I will never know. But I licked her one more time because I like this Mary so much. And because, yes, it *is* boring. This Mary knows her stuff!

I put my head back on the floor. Mary still needed to work on *her* settle. And you know what helps a human settle down and relax? Petting a dog! It's true. We learned it at Helper U. Every time a person scratches a dog's back or rubs a dog's tummy, "happy hormones" hit the person's brain and they feel better. Here's the cool thing: It makes dogs feel better too. Petting a dog is a real win-win.

Sure enough, each time Mary's hand ran down my back, the gasoline-smell of her nervousness grew fainter and fainter. I heard her heartbeat slow down too.

Mary settled down. Me too. I dozed off. But that doesn't matter. The smell of fresh peanut butter-banana muffins woke me right up.

CHAPTER 7

The peanut butter-banana muffins *were* for me!
Mary's mom found a recipe that worked well for
humans *and* dogs. (*Not* cats though. Ha!)

Amazing. This is the best family.

After the humans ate one and I ate two—and
then tried to sneak a third—Mary asked if she
could show me her room. Sounded good to me!

Tasha said sure. But before we left, Tasha
showed Mary the hand commands for "sit,"
"down," and "do-si-do." Mary performed the
commands pretty well. I, of course, played the
game perfectly.

Then Mary patted her leg and said "Sparky"
in a higher-pitched version of her scratchy voice.

We were off. I let her go first up the stairs. Not because I don't know where her room was—I could smell the hand sanitizer a mile away—but because it is considerate to let new friends go first.

That's Good Manners. (See: Trick #1.)

But halfway up the stairs—the part where the steps turn sharp to the left—we hit a snag. A cat-shaped snag, to be exact.

The gray cat smelled like tin foil and chicken. She arched her back and hissed like the cobra I'd seen on a TV show called *Scariest Snakes on Earth* with Tasha.

I stepped back. This cat was really scary!

Mary bent down toward the cobra-cat and slipped a hand under its arched tummy.

"Oh, Custard."

Custard! I've had custard—well, a few licks anyway. Custard is soft and sweet. That cat was no Custard!

But this was my big chance. If I was going to show Mary how to make new friends—and I was—I needed to show that I could be not afraid.

I put a front paw forward. Then a back paw. Two paws later, all four were square on the same landing as Mary and Custard, the Cobra-Cat.

I sat my Good Dog Sit and swung my tail into a wag. My tongue drooped out of my mouth.

Mary lowered Custard to where I sat and said, "See, Custy? This is Sparky. Isn't he sweet?"

I made my best silly face. There was no way this cat wouldn't want to be friends!

But Custard just laser-beamed me with her eyes again. She wanted me to look away. I knew it.

But my mind game was better than hers. I kept my loopy face, but I stared right back. *You will be my friend, Custard. You will be my friend. If for no other reason than because I really want to help Mary!*

I wish Learn to Read Minds could be Trick #3. But all my practice on Tasha has shown me humans will never quite master this. But cats? That's another story. They get it. When Custard unleashed her claws and swiped a paw at me, I knew: Custard read my mind.

Still, Custard was a tough cat to crack. Time to whip out some more Make New Friends Tricks.

"Be a nice girl," Mary said to Custard. "Let's go to my room and see if we can't all make friends."

Custard hissed at me again. I ignored her. I loved Mary's idea. Learning to make friends was the whole reason I was there, after all.

So I got to it. Took off running. I beat everyone up the rest of the stairs and trotted right toward Mary's room. I waited for her at the door.

"How'd you know which room was mine?" Mary asked. (It was early in our friendship. She didn't know of my brilliance yet.)

When Mary opened the door, I rushed

past her, which wasn't quite acting like the professional and polite dog I was trained to be. But I couldn't help it! As soon as the door swung open—*bam!*—a dry and dusty scent hit me. Dust mites! But not like the dust mites we have in Chicago. These must have been *Texas* dust mites. I could almost smell the cowboys and cow poop on them. I followed the scent right to a pile of stuffed animals. Ahh, my favorite.

I dug my snout into the pile of bears and bunnies, dogs and lambs. I honed in on a trim alligator. It fit perfectly in my mouth. I brought it to Mary who sat criss-cross applesauce on her bed. Custard sat next to her on a pillow.

"You found Allie," Mary said.

I did. I did find Allie. Now throw her! I'll find her again!

Mary could read my mind after all! She tossed Allie across the room. I just knew: this Mary is *the* best. She'll have no trouble making friends!

Mary tossed Allie again. The gator landed right in front of a window. How hadn't I noticed the window was open? I love an open window! Before snagging Allie off the ground, I lifted my nose for a quick sniff. Aah, a bird had been here. Robin. No…cardinal. And this was a maple tree. Nothing like the smell of sugary-sweet sap in the summertime. Well, except maybe the woodsy smell of squirrels.

I smelled three different squirrels on the breeze off this tree. I pushed my head further out the window.

"Careful," Mary said. "Don't want you to fall out. I'm not supposed to even have that window open. The screen's not in yet."

I pulled my head back in and scooped Allie off the floor.

When I brought Allie back to the bed, Mary patted her mattress. She's so smart. Tasha didn't even need to teach her this one! I noted where

Custard sat and planned my jump onto the bed. I landed perfectly. Right at Mary's feet. Two pillows away from Custard.

Mary scratched my head and leaned over to grab a picture from her nightstand.

"This is my dad," Mary said. I followed her finger as it tapped the picture. I wished pictures grabbed smells of the people and places in them. A dog can tell a lot more about a person that way.

"He stayed in Texas," Mary said. "With his new family. Just my mom and I moved up here. I miss him."

Sadness smells like salt. Tastes like it too. This was a salty moment.

I put my head in Mary's lap. She ran my ear through her fingers and sniffed. I listened hard as Mary told me about how she was sad about her dad and how scared she was about going to her new school and meeting new friends.

I wished I could tell Mary that my dad still lives somewhere in Wisconsin. With his other family. I wished I could tell her that I've never even met my dad but that I still missed him every day. And that sometimes I dream I'm running alongside him, poking my snout into sheep bottoms while he calls me a good boy and tells me that he's proud of me for being a world-famous Helper Hound.

And I wished I could tell Mary that I know it's scary to move somewhere new—and to feel

so alone and to think you'll never make friends.

I wanted to tell her: it's going to be OK (Trick #2). She'll be the best at making friends. She'll make a million new ones. I wanted to do this because Be A Good Listener and Be Willing to Share Your Heart is Trick #3. But it's hard for a dog to say all that in words.

So instead, I focused too hard on sending my thoughts into her brain, and a long, flutey toot escaped from under my tail. I was embarrassed, even though it felt good to let that go.

"Ew!" Mary said, and straightened up. Custard leapt off the bed.

Normally their reaction would have hurt my feelings, but Mary was laughing. And laughing is the *best*. Make someone laugh and you make a friend. That's Trick #4.

Even as Mary leaned back away from me,
I felt her body shake. In case you're wondering,
a good belly laugh normally smells like a
burp—like whatever you had for lunch.
But this time, the belly-laugh smell was
overpowered by the peanut butter-banana
muffins I had for snack. They smelled a lot
better going in than coming out.

Anyway, tooting in front of new friends is not polite, as Tasha says. However, if it gets people laughing, I think it's worth it.

Mary wiped her eyes and then slid out from under me. "Now I have to go to the bathroom," Mary said.

I followed her to the door of her room. She pulled it closed behind her and put her hand into something that looked like a "stay" command.

"Wait here with Custard until I get back," she said. "Try to get along."

I sat and swished my tail across her carpeted floor. The door clicked behind her.

CHAPTER 8

If I had been certain that Mary had told me to stay, I'd have stayed. I'd have sat my Good Dog Sit until Mary opened that door. But since I wasn't sure, I went ahead and jumped up on the bed, only turning around when Custard hissed behind me.

I brought my snout toward Custard's tiny black nose. If only she'd give me one little sniff, she'd know I'm a good dog! But Custard swiped at my nose with her sharp claw—ouch! —and then pranced to the windowsill.

She jumped up and lasered me again, daring or inviting me—depending on how you look at it—to come toward her.

So I did. I trotted my happy-go-luckiest trot right over to the window. And watched Custard leap right out.

I couldn't believe my eyes! Didn't Custard know it was a *long way down*?

She must not have. Because Custard YEEEOOWED as she wrapped her whole body around the thin branch closest to the window. The branch nodded under her weight.

I barked my best *Danger! Danger!* bark. But I stopped short when I remembered: I am a Helper Hound. Custard needed help. I could help!

I stretched my head as far out the window as I could. The tip of her tail was a Milk-Bone's length away from my snout. If she'd turn around, Custard could jump on my head and use me as a bridge. But she wouldn't turn around.

Custard's gray body shook as the branch bobbed and wobbled.

I hoped Custard could read my mind: *Inch forward. Inch forward,* I repeated. If she could read my mind, then once she got to the thicker part of the branch and then the trunk, I could guide her with my mind all the way down.

But Custard didn't budge. *Holy cow! What were we going to do?*

I thought of my dad. I often did that in a pinch. I pictured him in his full Border Collie glory, running and weaving alongside the sheep, herding them to go just where he wanted them. Herding Custard was no use. But then I pictured another sheepdog trick Tasha and I had seen on the show *Super Sheepdogs.*

Sometimes when strong stares and weaving and running didn't get the sheep where they'd want the sheep to go, a couple of quick snap-snaps of the teeth did the trick.

That was it! My teeth!

I plopped my front paws on the windowsill and stretched my whole body forward. My snout was now within a Kibble-and-Bit of Custard's tail. I watched as her tail swung from left, to right, and then *bam!* Right in front of my snout.

I snapped my snout forward. This time, my whole mouth clamped gently on her tail and I pulled her down the branch, closer to the window.

Custard *yeeeoow*ed the whole way until the moment she had to let go of the branch. I held tight but knew—from experience—that trusting someone you only just met and weren't all that sure you liked was not the easiest thing to do. But sometimes you have to trust somebody (this is Trick #5).

And Custard did. With one final *MEOW*,
she sprung her paws free from the branch and I
pulled her all the way back through the window.

It was like I was born to do this! (Ahem, Be
Yourself = Trick #6.)

I expected a hiss and a swat. But Custard surprised me. As I sat my Good Dog Sit in front of the open window, Custard purred and snaked her body along mine. Custard rubbed her face on my neck just as Mary opened the door.

"Wow!" Mary said. "How did you two become such good friends?"

Mary knelt on the floor and scratched us both. Her eyebrows scrunched when she pulled a leaf out of Custard's fur.

"What on earth...?"

Then Mary looked out the window. "Custard, tell me you weren't out there."

Just then, something caught in my throat. I coughed and coughed and finally spit out a small, wet tuft of gray fur. And a leaf.

Mary grabbed it before it could hit the rug. She tilted her head toward me and said, "Is this Custard's? Were you in the tree too?"

I barked. What else could I do?

Mary laughed and said something about wishing she could've been a fly on the wall. I hate flies so I was glad she wasn't.

Although, maybe now that I know how to make friends with cats (Be Memorable! Trick #7), I could probably make friends with flies too.

But that would have to wait for another day,

because it was time to head home. I was sad to leave. I liked Mary! And, believe it or not, I liked Custard too. Sshh, that's *our* secret.

Tasha and I went back to visit Mary the next day. We all walked to the playground at her school for Meet the Teachers.

Mary was nervous. I could feel it through my leash.

"You okay?" Mary's mom asked.

Mary took a deep breath and reached down to pet me.

"Yeah," Mary said. "I'll do just what Sparky showed me with Custard."

Mary's mom smiled. "Remember to relax and use your manners," she said.

Even Mary's mom knew my tricks!

Mary and I walked to the playground. Mary's mom and Tasha stayed a few steps behind.

A girl walked up and asked to pet me. Mary

nodded and put out her hand. The girl smiled and shook Mary's hand.

"I'm Jazmine," she said. "Are you the new girl? I was the new girl last year."

Then Jazmine knelt down to pet me. Mary did too. They talked about teachers and lunches and cats. They giggled when I rolled over and scratched my own back on the blacktop.

More kids came by and Mary shook lots of hands. She laughed and listened and was kind and so brave. She got through almost all my tricks right there on the playground.

A bell rang. It was time to go meet her teachers—and time for Tasha and me to head home.

Mary hugged me goodbye and handed my leash to Tasha. Jazmine grabbed her hand and they ran off across the playground together. Off to a new adventure!

I barked, Tasha waved, and Mary's mom

sniffled. I licked her hand.

"Hope she's okay," Mary's mom said.

Mary would be just fine. She knew all my
best tricks. Mary was going to make a million
friends.

EPILOGUE

Dear Sparky:

My first day of school went really well. I was so scared when my mom said good-bye. I had to stand in line by myself! So I thought about you and how petting you made me feel better. And that helped! I felt better just imagining I was petting you.

Then I saw that girl, Jazmine, who we met on the playground. Remember her? She said you were super cute. Anyway, Jazmine isn't in my class, but she said we could play at recess. And we did! Maybe we can all play together when you come to visit next week.

My teacher, Mr. Jefferson, is really nice. He told everyone I'd just moved from Texas. Then Todd, the boy next to me, said he moved from Texas two years ago! Todd wanted to know if we still had rattlesnakes in Texas. I said we did, and told the story of how my dad found one curled up by the pool once, and the kids all screamed. Todd and I laughed.

Most of the kids seem nice. One girl seems kind of mean. I smile at her and she just looks away. I thought maybe we won't be friends. But then I remembered you and Custard. Miracles happen, right? Hahaha.

I'm baking more peanut butter banana muffins for when you come next week. Can't wait.

Love,

Mary

Sparkplug's
7 Tried-and-True Tricks
for Making Friends

TRICK #1: Use your manners. Good manners are never just about being fancy. Good manners are *always* about being considerate or putting other people first. It shows people that we care when we do things like hold a door open or send a thank-you note. Even *table manners*—not smacking our food and remembering to put our napkins in our laps—show love to the people around us.

TRICK #2: Settle down. Remember, it's going to be OK. Starting a new school or moving to a new neighborhood can be scary. We worry that the kids won't like us and that we'll miss our old friends terribly. This is normal. Everyone worries about this (even the kids you think don't!). But we can also let our imaginations get the best of us when we imagine the *worst thing that could happen*. What about imagining the *best things*? It takes time to make new friends, but we don't have to worry. When we feel afraid, it helps to practice our settle: sit on the floor with a real pet or furry stuffed animal and breathe in and out while petting the animal. Remember, it's all going to be OK.

TRICK #3: Be a good listener and share your heart.
Everybody needs someone to talk to. So one of
the best ways to make good friends and to *be*
a good friend is by being a good, trustworthy
listener. When we want to make a good friend,
we can ask questions and then listen carefully
to the answers or the stories. Then we can also
share things about ourselves. It can be scary!
But by sharing funny or sad or embarrassing
stories from our own lives, we help make new
friends feel comfortable being themselves
around us.

TRICK #4: Make 'em laugh! Todd and Mary
became friends because they were able to laugh
together. There's nothing quite like sharing a
joke or a funny story or giggling that brings
friends together. The library is full of great
joke books for those of us who need a little
silly inspiration.

TRICK #5: Trust somebody. We all worry that other people are going to hurt our feelings. And know what? It does happen to all of us! No one goes through life without getting their feelings hurt. Sometimes our feelings get hurt because we have to move. Other times, kids say or do something mean. But just like Custard had to trust Sparky, we have to trust other people once in a while. This means when someone tries to reach out to us, we can reach back.

TRICK #6: Be yourself! It's easy to try to make friends by changing who we are and pretending to be someone we aren't or to like something we don't. Be willing to be you! Be weird if you're weird. Be funny if you're funny. Be creative if you're creative. Be smart if you're smart. Be athletic if you're athletic. Be brave if you're brave. Be all those things and more if it means being yourself.

TRICK #7: Go on adventures and create memories together! We don't need to go on a safari or discover new worlds to go on adventures. Adventures are all around—even right on the playground. But one of the best ways to make friends is to have fun—play, pretend, explore, and make a million memories.

FUN FACTS

About Border Collies and Bernese Mountain Dogs

Sparky is a mixed breed, or a mutt. That means his parents were not the same breed. In the story, Sparky's father is a Border Collie and his mother is a Bernese. Mountain Dog. These two breeds are very different from each other. But they came together to make Sparky a special dog.

Sparky is smart and likes to work hard. Those are qualities of a Border Collie. These dogs get their name because they originally came from the border of Scotland and England. All Border Collies are descended from one dog named Old Hemp, who was born in 1893. Old Hemp herded sheep. Unlike other herding dogs, he was gentle but he could still show those sheep who was boss!

Border Collie

Border collies are very smart dogs. If they cannot keep busy with work or play, they get bored. And a bored Border Collie can get into a lot of trouble! Some Border Collies on farms still herd sheep. But most people don't have sheep for their dogs to herd. That's why many Border Collies take part in games called agility (*uh-jil-uh-tee*) trials. These are tests that let a dog run, jump, and race around obstacles. Border collies also like to play with toys and go on long walks and runs.

What about Sparky's other half, the Bernese Mountain Dog? These dogs are big and beautiful. They originally come from Switzerland, and some experts think the breed might be more than 2,000 years old. Because these dogs are so big and strong, they were once used to pull carts. A Bernese Mountain Dog can pull up to 1,000 pounds. They also make great herding dogs and guard dogs. They are great pets, too, if you have the space.

Bernese Mountain Dog

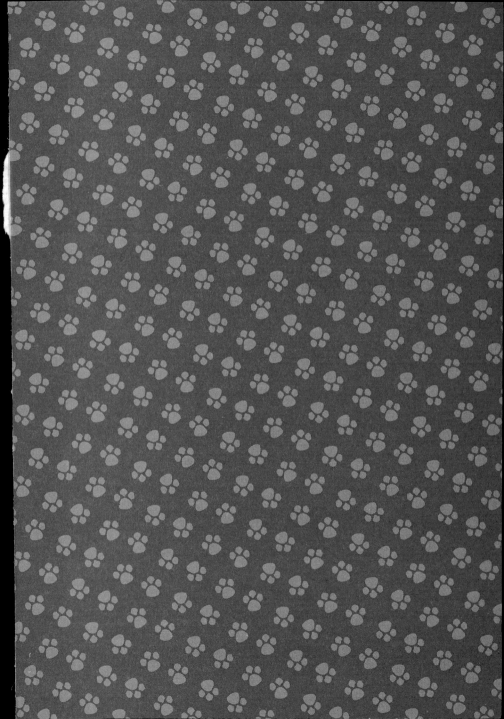